# A BOY AND HIS MIRROR

Marchánt Davis

Illustrated by Keturah A. Bobo

Nancy Paulsen Books

To every niece and nephew. Every kid from Nicetown and beyond. To Demara, Kareem, and Nick. This is for you.
May you look into your mirror with joy and pride, and may each and every one of your flowers bloom. —M. D.

To all the magical Black boys.
To my son and muse, Mekhi, and my nephews, Ari and Uriah. ❤ —K. A. B.

**Nancy Paulsen Books**
An imprint of Penguin Random House LLC, New York

First published in the United States of America by Nancy Paulsen Books,
an imprint of Penguin Random House LLC, 2023

Text copyright © 2023 by Marchánt Davis
Illustrations copyright © 2023 by Art by Keturah Ariel LLC

Nancy Paulsen Books and colophon are trademarks of Penguin Random House LLC.

Visit us online at penguinrandomhouse.com.

Library of Congress Cataloging-in-Publication Data is available.

Manufactured in China

ISBN 9780593110553

1 3 5 7 9 10 8 6 4 2

TOPL

Edited by Nancy Paulsen | Art direction by Cecilia Yung | Design by Cindy De la Cruz
Text set in Javeira
The illustrations were created with acrylic on board and Procreate.

Once upon a time, there was a boy named Chris—
who had this hair no one could miss.

It was long and curly.
(Some kids called it girly.)
But Chris liked it—
"Hey, it's a real good fit!"

Some kids laughed. Some liked to stare.

*Dang,* Chris thought, *it's only hair!*

His mom said, "Kids sure do like to tease,
but if *you* like it, try to feel at ease."

Chris walked by the mirror, checked out the view.
Took a deeper look. Would it offer a clue?

And then, right there, a woman appeared.
It was kind of wild and a little weird!

"In a faraway land, child,
  you'd look like a king.
 They'd love you just as you are—
  tell you, 'Don't change a thing.'"

"Who ARE you?"

"No, who are YOU?!
 That's the question—
  so what will you do?"

So Chris decided he'd act like a king.
That just might work—it'd be his new thing.

He strolled right on by, showing bling, acting cool.

But the kids didn't get it. Some were still kinda cruel.

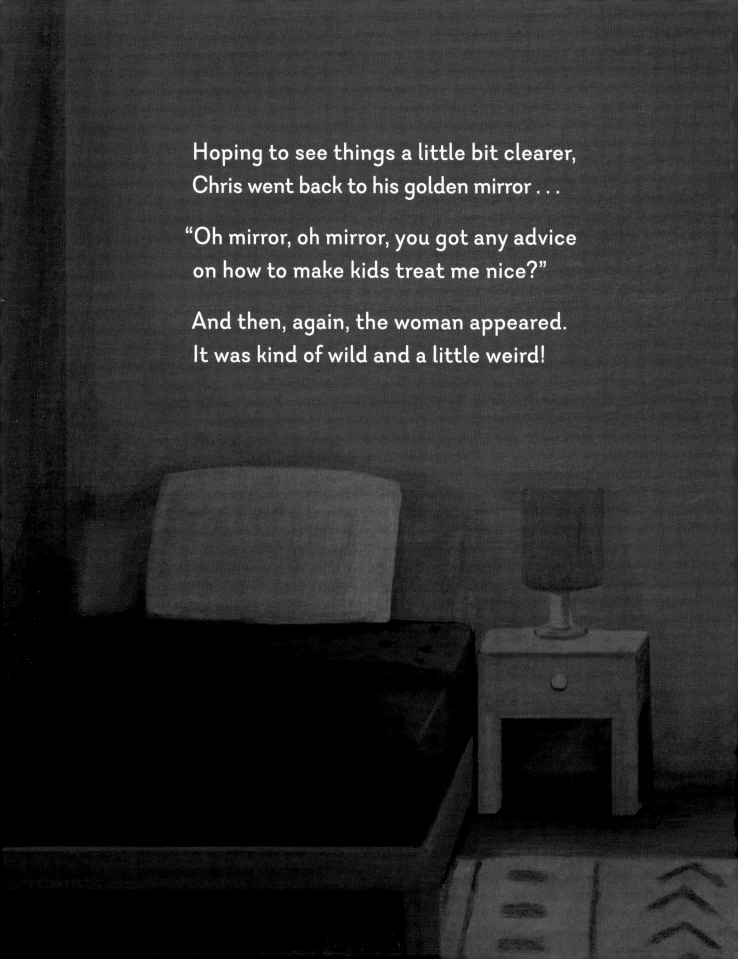

Hoping to see things a little bit clearer,
Chris went back to his golden mirror . . .

"Oh mirror, oh mirror, you got any advice
on how to make kids treat me nice?"

And then, again, the woman appeared.
It was kind of wild and a little weird!

It's not about swagger, it's not about bling.
You're a kid who's kind and extremely smart.
Try showing them what's in your mind—and your great big heart."

At recess, Chris announced he had something to say.
Told those kids, "I think there's a better way.

How 'bout we stop judging, quit calling names.
Be a little more chill. Stop playing games.

And one more thing I wanna say to you . . .

"My hair is amazing—and yours is too!"

Then Chris was real happy to hear
a bunch of kids giving a cheer.

Even better, one kid told Chris,
"I like what you said—it's no fun when kids dis.
The reason I never came up to you
was I thought maybe you were *too* cool!

Now I get we're all good in our own way.
So thanks for that. Now how 'bout we play!"

"I wanna play too!" "Don't forget about me!"
And when Chris looked up, one kid turned to three!

Chris beamed out a smile to all his new friends,
and they all played together till recess's end.

Back at his mirror at the end of the day,
Chris was real happy and had something to say.

"Oh mirror, oh mirror, with your golden bling,
I tried what you said. I did a new thing!
I walked like a king—*and* I was nice.
So thanks for all the good advice."

His mom said, "Chris! I'm glad you figured it out.
You're the perfect you, without a doubt."

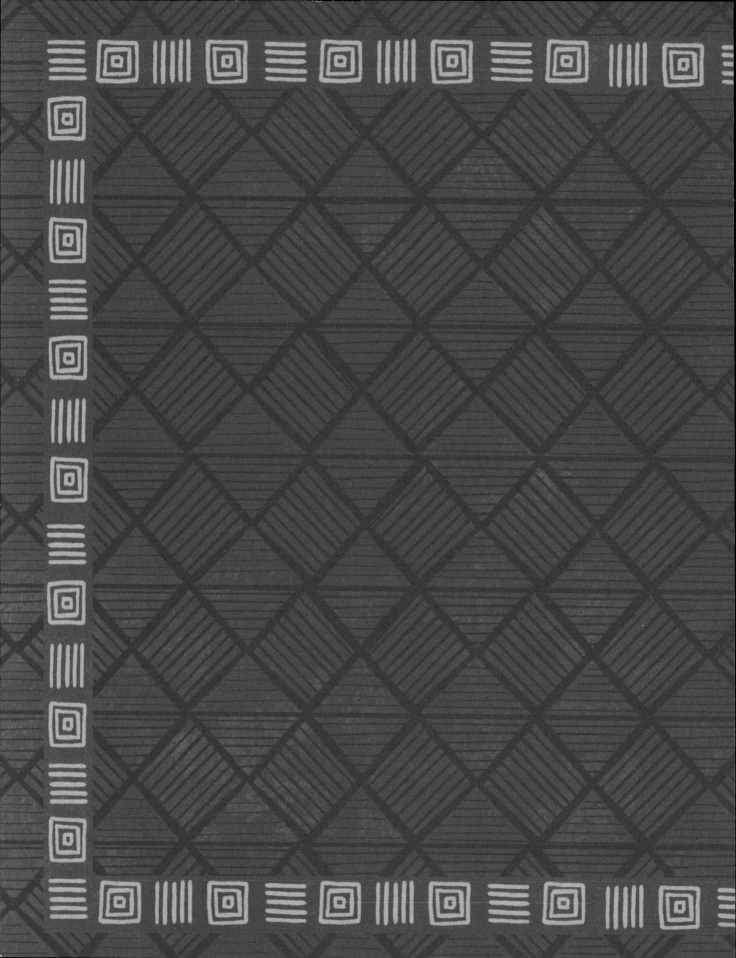